For Dill the dog

With special thanks to Sarah Whittick and Terry Donovan

Copyright © 2000 by David Ellwand

All rights reserved.

CIP Data is available.

Published in the United States 2000 by Dutton Children's Books,

a division of Penguin Putnam Books for Young Readers

345 Hudson Street, New York, New York 10014

http://www.penguinputnam.com

Designed by Alan Carr

Printed in Hong Kong · First Edition

ISBN 0-525-46385-2

1 3 5 7 9 10 8 6 4 2

ALFRED'S PARTY

A Collection of Picture Puzzles by

DAVID ELLWAND

DUTTON CHILDREN'S BOOKS · NEW YORK

Alfred woke up one morning with a funny feeling—a feeling that he had forgotten something very important. Alfred often felt like this. He was a *very* forgetful dog.

Then suddenly he remembered—it was his birthday! He wanted to have a party. First, Alfred needed to make invitations for all his friends. He couldn't have a party without invitations! But where was Alfred's pen?

Turn the page to help Alfred find his pen.

crown, a chess piece, a robot clock, some

Inside his messy desk, Alfred found lots of pencils, a little gold plastic scissors, a ring, a shovel, and . . .

his favorite pen!

It's my birthday.
Please come to
my party tonight.

Woof,
Alfred

Alfred made six party invitations and delivered them to all his friends. Then he trotted home.

Next, Alfred needed to make a birthday cake. He couldn't have a party without a cake! But where was Alfred's mixing bowl? *Turn the page to help Alfred find his blue mixing bowl.*

In his messy kitchen,

a red prize ribbon, and . . .

his favorite mixing bowl!

Alfred was a forgetful dog, but he was also a splendid baker. He mixed and measured and tasted and tested until the birthday cake was just right. By that time, he was covered in flour. He couldn't go to a party looking like that! He needed a bath, but where was Alfred's bath brush? *Turn the page to help Alfred find his bath brush.*

a yellow taxi, three boats, a pair of goggles,

In the cupboard where he kept his rubber ducks, Alfred found

a wooden doll, a balloon, and . . .

his favorite bath brush!

Alfred scrubbed his fur and soaked in the warm suds for a while. Then he jumped out of the tub and shook himself from nose to tail.

It was time to decorate the house and set the table. He couldn't have a party without decorations and party favors! But where were Alfred's party hats?

Turn the page to help Alfred find the party hats.

an apple, a spool of thread, a diamond necklace,

In his jumble of party decorations, Alfred found

a string of beads, a little rocking horse, and . . .

six fancy party hats!

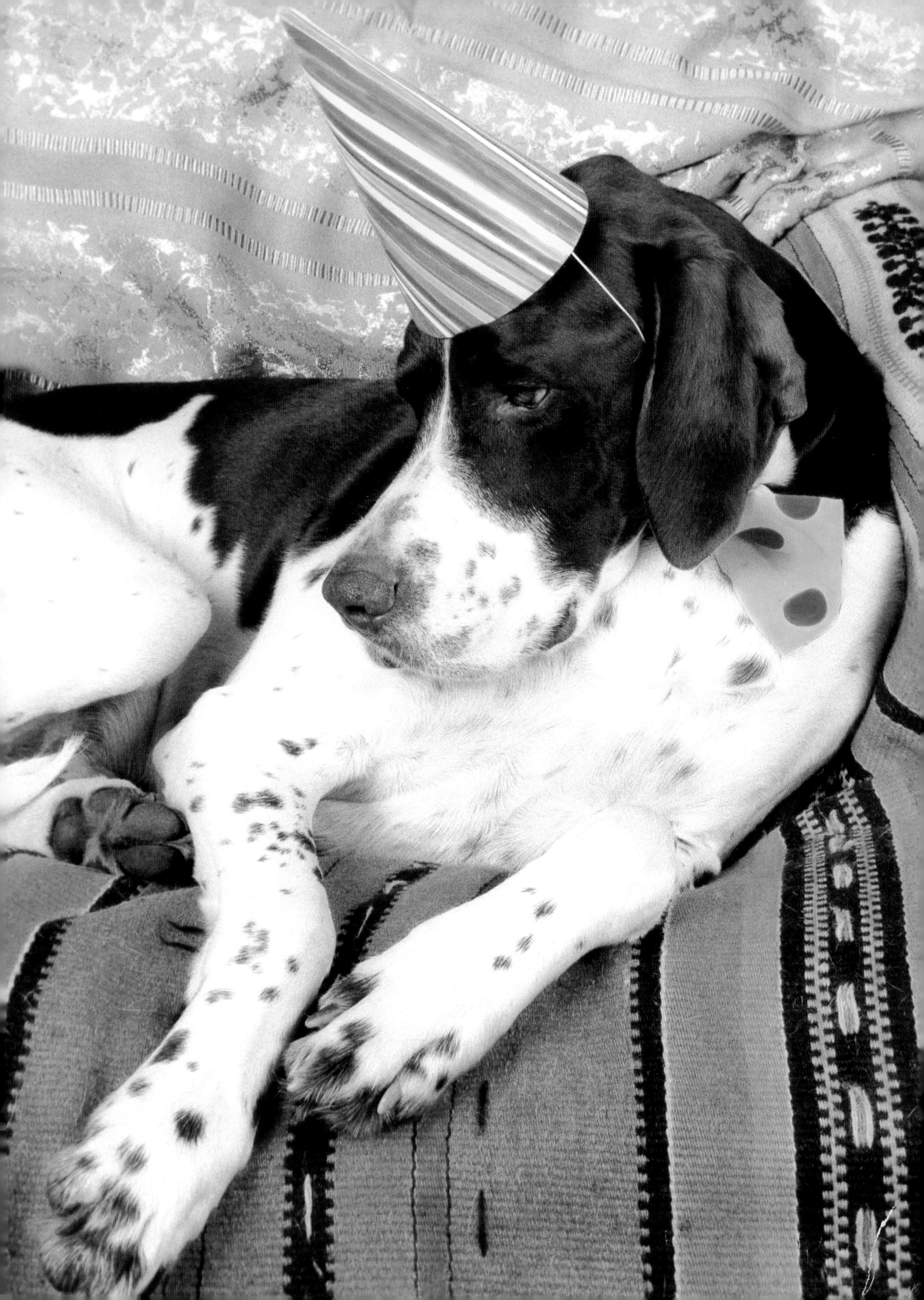

Alfred set the table, hung up the streamers, blew up the balloons, and put on his party hat. Then he waited. And waited. And waited. Everything was ready for Alfred's party, but where were all his guests? He couldn't have a party without guests!

Turn the page to help Alfred find his friends.

"HERE we are, Alfred! We would never forget your birthday!" barked Alfred's friends. Even the cat came to the party (although she hadn't been invited). Everyone howled a happy birthday song. They ate cake and played

games like Hide the Leash and Chew the Shoe. Then
Alfred opened his presents, but there was so much
wrapping paper left over that he couldn't find them!
Turn the page to help Alfred find his birthday presents.

Alfred found his presents—a wooden airplane,

Hidden in the crumpled paper and rumpled ribbons,

a rawhide dog bone, an abacus, a garden gnome,

a bow tie, and a teddy bear.

When all of his guests had gone home,
Alfred admired his new gifts.

"Almost-forgotten birthdays are the best
kind," Alfred thought to himself.
"But they are certainly
a lot of work."

Here are some things that forgetful Alfred *didn't* find. Did *you*?